The DINOSAUR Files

THE RISE OF THE REPTILES

text by Olivia Brookes

New York

Published in 2012 by Windmill Books, an imprint of Rosen Publishing
29 East 21st Street, New York, NY 10010

Illustrated by Julius T. Csotonyi, Steve Kirk, Simon Mendez, Nicki Palin, Peter Scott, John Sibbick, and Studio Inklink

Library of Congress Cataloging-in-Publication Data

Brookes, Olivia.
The rise of the reptiles / by Olivia Brookes.
p. cm. — (The dinosaur files)
Includes index.
ISBN 978-1-61533-519-0 (library binding) — ISBN 978-1-61533-526-8 (pbk.) — ISBN 978-1-61533-527-5 (6-pack)
1. Dinosaurs—Juvenile literature. 2. Dinosaurs—Juvenile literature I. Title.
QE861.5.B7569 2012
567.9—dc23
2011022840

Printed and bound in Malaysia

Websites

For Web resources related to the subject of this book, go to: www.windmillbooks.com/weblinks and select this book's title.

CPSIA Compliance Information: Batch #OW2102WM: For further information contact Windmill Books, New York, New York at 1-866-478-0556.

Contents

Introduction

Today's lizards, snakes, crocodiles, and other reptiles come from a group of animals that once ruled Earth for 250 million years— much longer than the mammals have been in charge (that's just 65 million years and counting). At first, these creatures were small and lizardlike. They lived in swamps in the Late Carboniferous period. When the world became drier in the Permian period, they moved onto land and slowly became more like the reptiles we know today.

Some of these reptiles evolved into dinosaurs and became the largest animals that ever roamed Earth. Other kinds developed wings, becoming the first backboned animals to fly. Still others took to the water and, over time, became gigantic predators of the sea.

The first part of this book tells the amazing story of how the reptiles came to rule Earth. The second part focuses on the flying and marine reptiles that lived alongside the dinosaurs. Much more information about the dinosaurs themselves can be found in other titles in *The Dinosaur Files* series.

Geologic Time

EARTH is 4,600 million years old. Earth's history is measured in geologic time: spans of millions of years. A "recent" event in geologic time may have happened in the last 1 million years.

Geologic time is split into periods (right). Dinosaurs lived during the Triassic, Jurassic, and Cretaceous periods. They first appeared about 230 million years ago. But life began more than 3,500 million years earlier. During that time, many kinds of plants and animals lived and died out. Mountains grew up and wore down. Sea levels rose and fell. Even the continents moved very, very slowly around the globe.

million years ago	Period	Events
	QUATERNARY	*First modern humans*
1.8	TERTIARY	*Dinosaurs extinct*
65	CRETACEOUS	*First flowering plants*
144	JURASSIC	*First birds*
208	TRIASSIC	*First mammals* *First dinosaurs*
245	PERMIAN	*First archosaurs*
286	CARBONIFEROUS	*First mammal-like reptiles* *First reptiles* *First amphibians*
360	DEVONIAN	*First lobefin fish* *First insects*
408	SILURIAN	*First fish with jaws* *First land plants*
438	ORDOVICIAN	*First jawless fish*
505	CAMBRIAN	*First shellfish*
550	PRECAMBRIAN	*Oldest fossils*
3,500		
4,600		*Formation of Earth*

If we could squeeze 4,600 million years of Earth's history into just 12 hours, the Precambrian period would take 10 hours 30 minutes. From the first living things to the present day would take up 1 hour 30 minutes (the dinosaurs died out just 9 minutes ago!). All of human history took place in the last second.

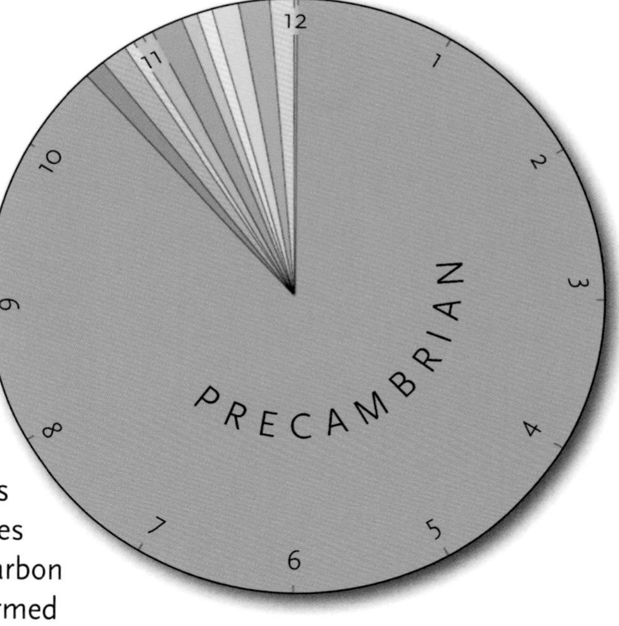

EARTH: THE EARLY YEARS

Just a few million years after Earth was born, volcanoes erupted, blasting gases into the air. These gases, hydrogen, carbon dioxide, water vapor, and nitrogen, formed Earth's atmosphere. When the water vapor cooled, clouds formed. Soon, rain began to fall. It rained for thousands of years, filling up the great basins in the land to make Earth's great oceans.

The First Living Things

THE FIRST LIFE ON EARTH probably appeared about 3,800 million years ago. No one knows how it began, but the first creatures lived in the oceans. There was not enough oxygen in the air on land for creatures to breathe. Ultraviolet radiation (rays from the Sun that cause sunburn) was at deadly levels.

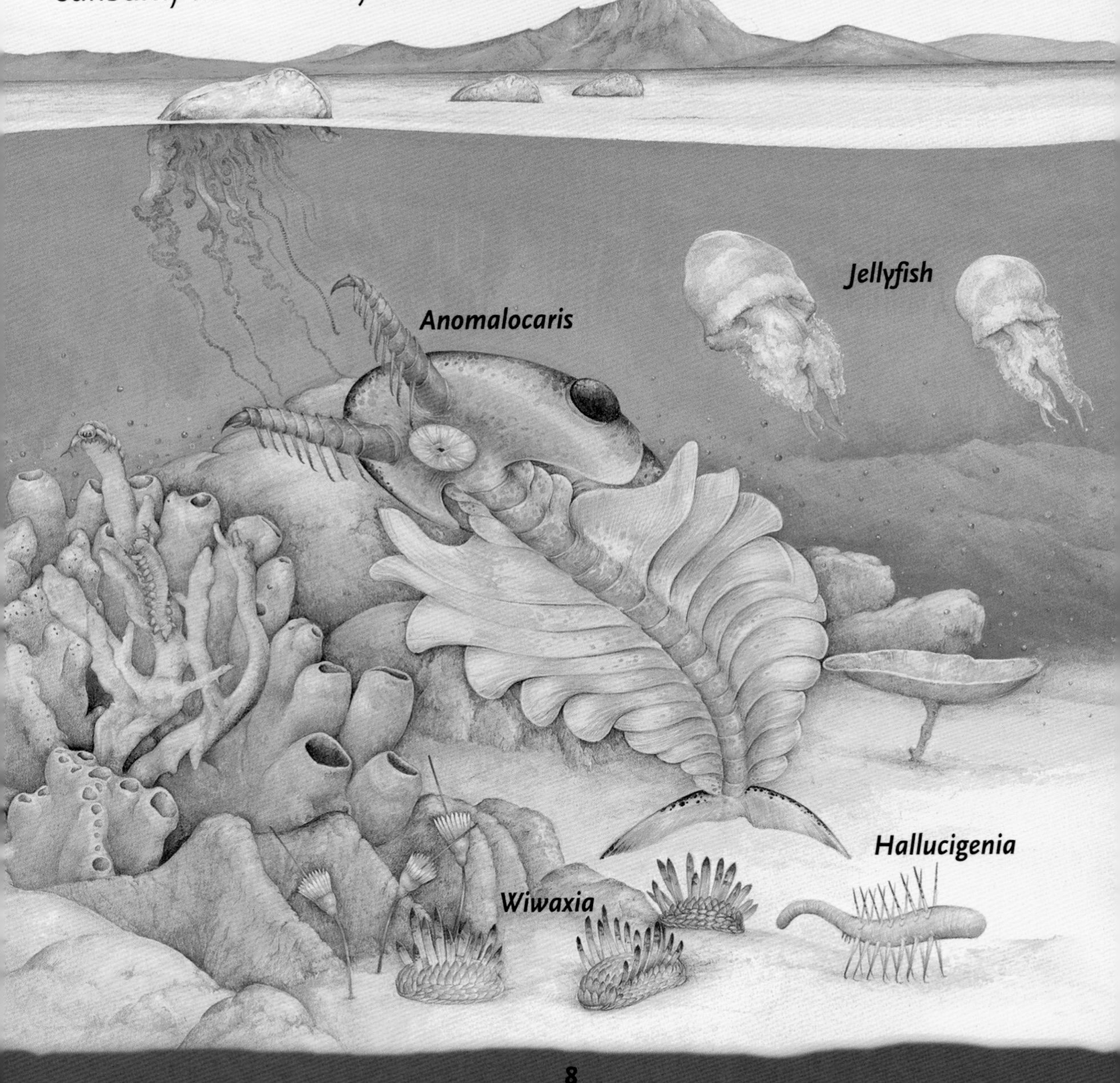

The earliest life forms were simple bacteria. It took a very, very long time (2,500 million years) for more complex life to develop. The first aquatic animals with shells or skeletons, such as shellfish, corals, and starfish, appeared 570 million years ago. Then, 550 million years ago, many new and different life forms appeared suddenly in an "explosion of life."

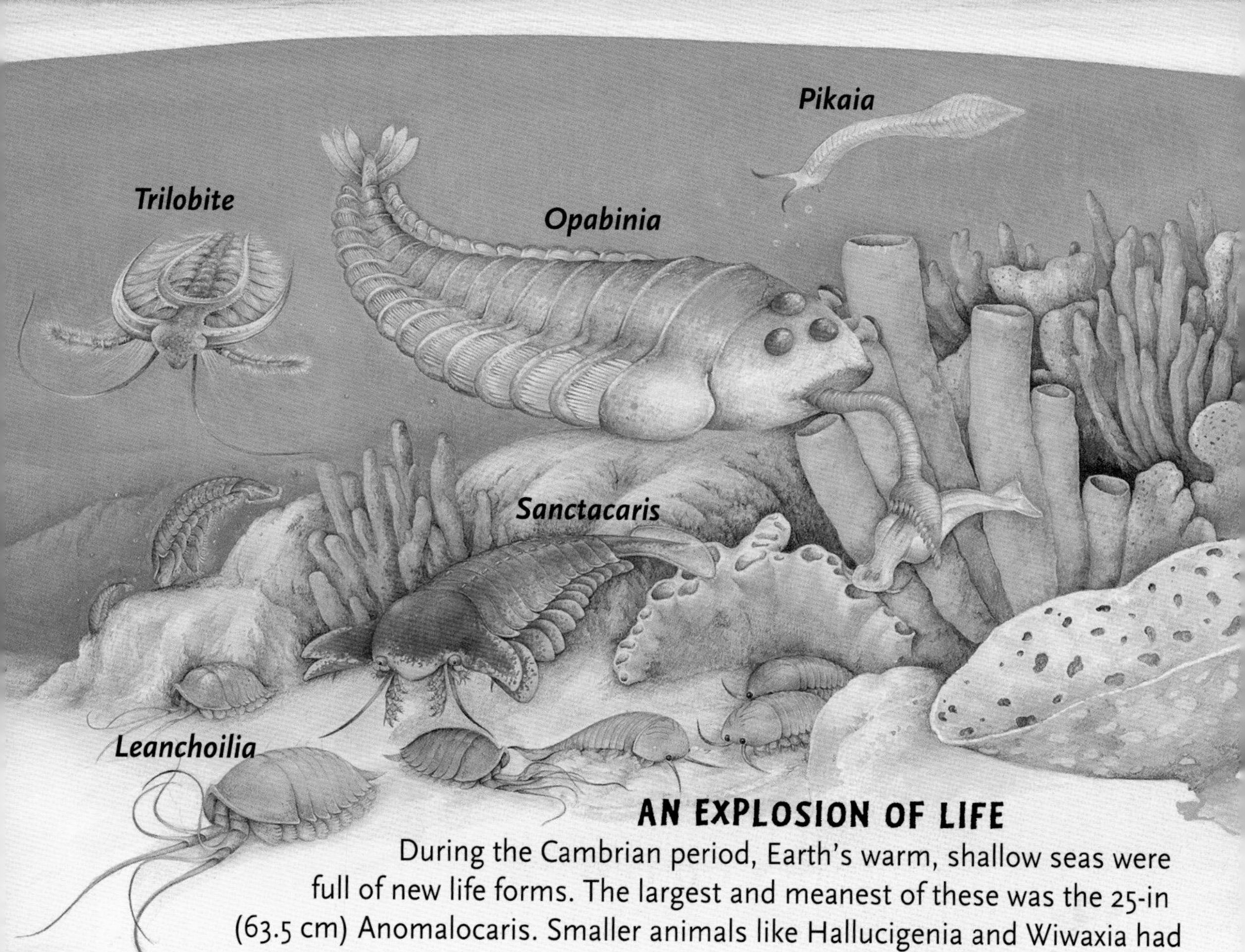

AN EXPLOSION OF LIFE

During the Cambrian period, Earth's warm, shallow seas were full of new life forms. The largest and meanest of these was the 25-in (63.5 cm) Anomalocaris. Smaller animals like Hallucigenia and Wiwaxia had to protect themselves from such predators. Pikaia, a small worm-like creature, had a rod running down its back. It was probably an early ancestor of vertebrates (animals with backbones), including fish, reptiles, birds, and mammals today.

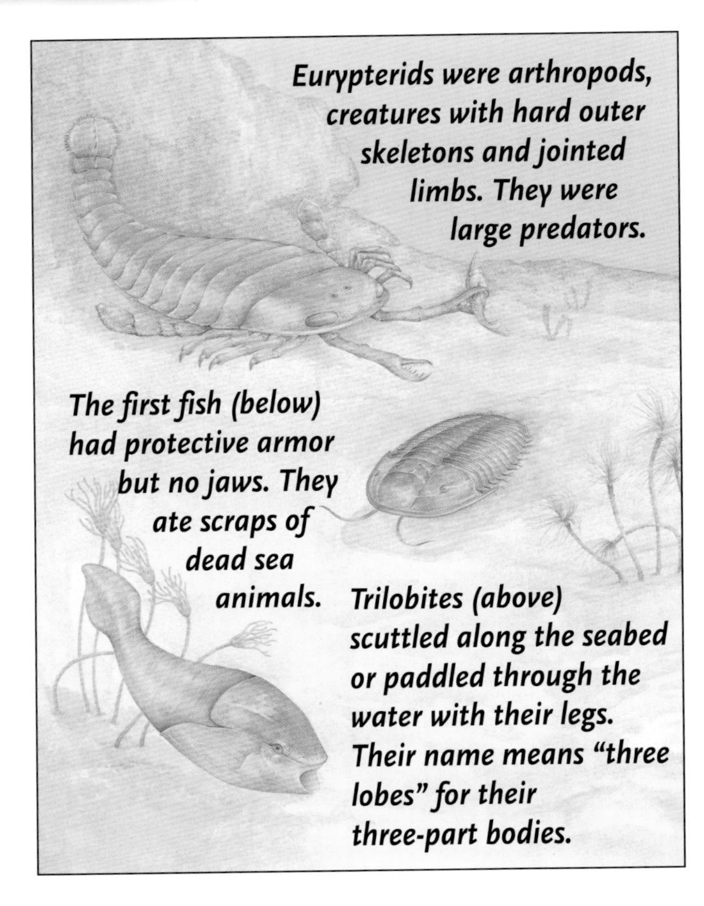

Eurypterids were arthropods, creatures with hard outer skeletons and jointed limbs. They were large predators.

The first fish (below) had protective armor but no jaws. They ate scraps of dead sea animals.

Trilobites (above) scuttled along the seabed or paddled through the water with their legs. Their name means "three lobes" for their three-part bodies.

FISH evolved rapidly during the Silurian and Devonian periods. The earliest fish had no fins or jaws, but once they had developed these, they became active predators. Two types of fish emerged. The first group had hard, bony skeletons and lived in seas and freshwater rivers. The second group had soft cartilage skeletons, like sharks have today.

FIRST LIFE ON LAND

Until about 450 million years ago, nothing lived on land. Then, tiny living things, called algae, began to be washed ashore during low tides. Land plants probably adapted over time. They developed waxy skin to stay moist and grew roots to fix themselves in the ground. By the late Ordovician period, plants were thriving on land.

These plants became food for some marine creatures that managed to clamber ashore: arthropods. Their shells kept them wet and their jointed legs were good on the uneven ground. Spiders and insects were the first land dwellers.

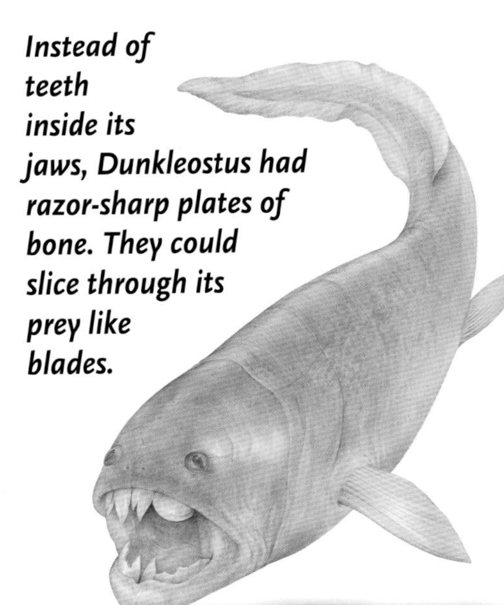

Instead of teeth inside its jaws, Dunkleostus had razor-sharp plates of bone. They could slice through its prey like blades.

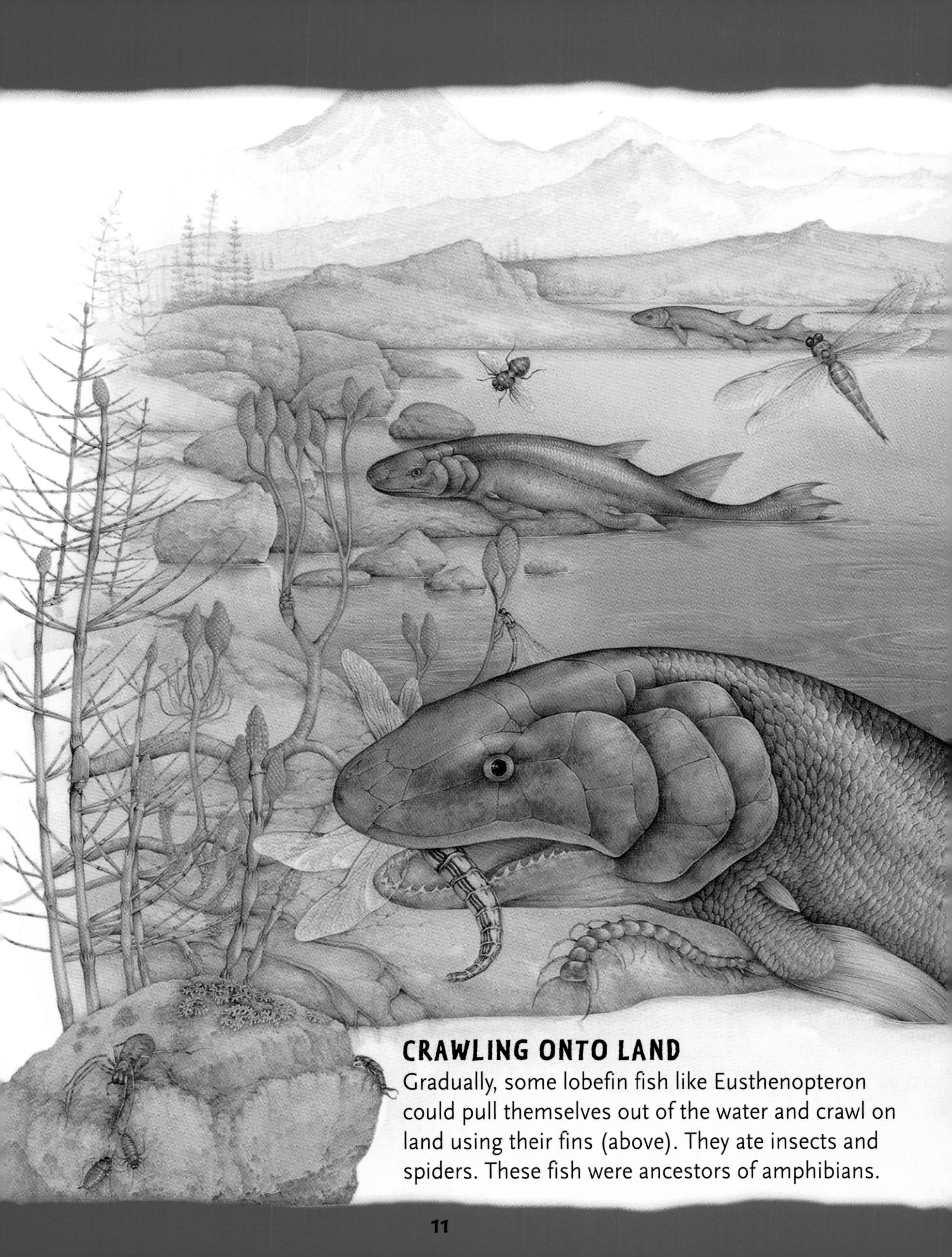

CRAWLING ONTO LAND

Gradually, some lobefin fish like Eusthenopteron could pull themselves out of the water and crawl on land using their fins (above). They ate insects and spiders. These fish were ancestors of amphibians.

Coal Swamps

BY THE BEGINNING of the Carboniferous period, plants had spread across the world's continents. Giant trees, such as Lepidendron (club moss) and Calamites (a large horsetail) filled the hot, steamy jungle swamps. Here, trees grew, died, and rotted. The dead matter eventually turned into a dense, dark soil called peat. Over millions of years, these beds of peat became squashed under other soil layers and became rock. Today, we call this rock coal.

In North America 300 million years ago, a group of Eryops, 6-ft- (2 m) long amphibians, wade ashore in the coal swamp. These heavy creatures probably spent most of their time in the water.

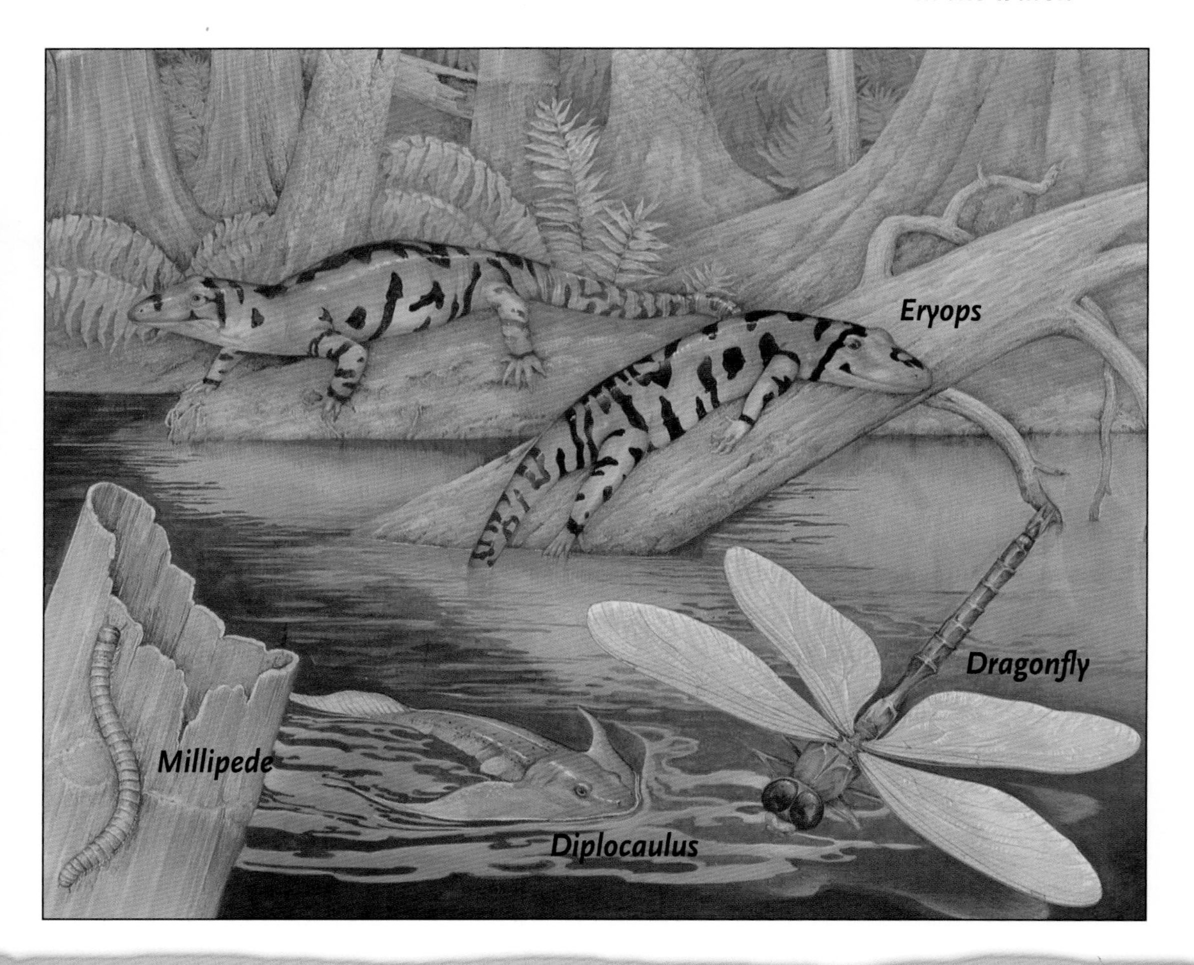

Hylonomus, or "forest mouse," looks down on Eryops.

In the coal swamps, dragonflies were the size of pigeons. Giant cockroaches and 6-foot- (2 m) long millipedes lived among the trees. Lurking in the waters were the first amphibians. Ichthyostega had a fish-like head and tail. It could crawl ashore to feed, but it still laid its eggs in water. Over millions of years, some amphibians became able to reproduce on land. They did not need to return to the water. These were the first reptiles. Hylonomus, an 8-inch- (20 cm) long, lizard-like creature, was one of them. It adapted to life on land by laying hard-shelled eggs.

Permian World

DURING the Permian period, there was just one large area of land: the "super-continent" of Pangaea. The southern parts of Pangaea, at the South Pole, were covered by a massive ice cap. Much of Earth's water was frozen in this ice, while the rest of the world's climate became very hot and dry. The hot, steamy jungles of the Carboniferous period were now vast scrublands and deserts. Large amphibians that depended on water for their jelly-like eggs started to die out. Reptiles, which laid their eggs on dry land, multiplied. They also developed powerful jaws, perfect for eating tough desert plants.

GIANT SAILS

Synapsid reptiles were ancestors of mammals. The earliest group were called pelycosaurs. Some were giants with huge sails on their backs, like Dimetrodon and Edaphosaurus. These sails were made of skin held up by long, thin spines along the animals' back. Scientists think the sails kept their bodies at the right temperature, warming them up in the sun and cooling them off when they were too hot.

Dimetrodon, a pelycosaur, basks in the sun.

Edaphosaurus

Dimetrodon

Varanosaurus

Ophiacodon

In the late Permian, there were many large synapsids, but diapsids were on the rise.

Three types of land reptiles ruled the dry Permian world. Anapsids (ancestors of tortoises and turtles) had a solid skull. Synapsids (ancestors of mammals) had one hole on each side of their skull. Diapsids had two holes on each side. This group were the ancestors of lizards, snakes, and crocodiles — and dinosaurs.

SLOW MOVERS

After pelycosaurs came lumbering animals like Moschops and Scutosaurus. Diapsids, like Protorosaurus and Coelurosauravus, were still rare.

Reptiles of Land, Sea, and Air

IN THE EARLY TRIASSIC PERIOD, a large number of sea and land animals became extinct. Scientists are not sure why this happened, though the extreme hot and dry climate across Pangaea could have been the cause. But some reptiles survived, including the mammal-like ones, such as Lystrosaurus, a pig-like reptile with tusks. Another group, the archosaurs, quickly multiplied. At first they had a low, sprawling gait, like lizards. Eventually, some of these animals began to walk more upright. The powerful runner Ornithosuchus, for example, had a short body with strong hind legs and a long balancing tail. By the late Triassic, some archosaurs were walking on two legs all the time. They were the first dinosaurs.

ALMOST A DINOSAUR

Euparkeria was a small archosaur with a slim body, a long tail, and long hind legs. Although it walked on all fours, it probably ran on two legs. It had needle-like teeth and liked to eat insects and small animals on the forest floor.

Euparkeria

Thrinaxodon

Thrinaxodon (left) was a cynodant, a mammal-like reptile about the size of a cat. Like a mammal, it digested food quickly, which raised its body temperature. Its fur coat kept this heat in. But its skeleton was like a reptile's and it laid eggs.

For the next 165 million years, dinosaurs ruled the land, while other kinds of reptiles dominated the sea and air. The marine reptiles were quite similar to dinosaurs. They had large eyes, sharp teeth, four limbs, and a tail. But instead of legs, they had flippers for swimming. The first marine reptiles, like Placodus and Nothosaurus (below), waddled around on land, but spent time in water diving for food. Over millions of years, new kinds evolved that lived in water all of the time (see pages 26-31).

Eudimorphodon

HIGH FLIERS

Another group of archosaurs could fly. They were called pterosaurs and included the rhamphorynchs and the pterodactyls (see pages 20-25). Eudimorphodon was one of the first pterosaurs. Its wings were sheets of skin stretching from its legs to its long fourth finger.

Placodus ate shellfish from the seabed, but its legs, feet, and claws were more useful on land. Nothosaurus had a long, slim body, and webbed hands and feet, perfect for swimming.

The Dinosaurs

DINOSAURS were land reptiles that lived in tropical habitats in the Triassic, Jurassic, and Cretaceous periods. Walking upright on two or four legs, most had long tails and scaly skin, but some had feathers. Some were as small as a duck while others were 75-ton (68 t) giants.

Other reptiles, like the Komodo dragon (left), walk with their legs splayed to the side. Dinosaurs stood upright with their legs beneath their bodies. Some, like , Compsognathus (right), could run very fast.

Dinosaurs from different continents in the Jurassic age

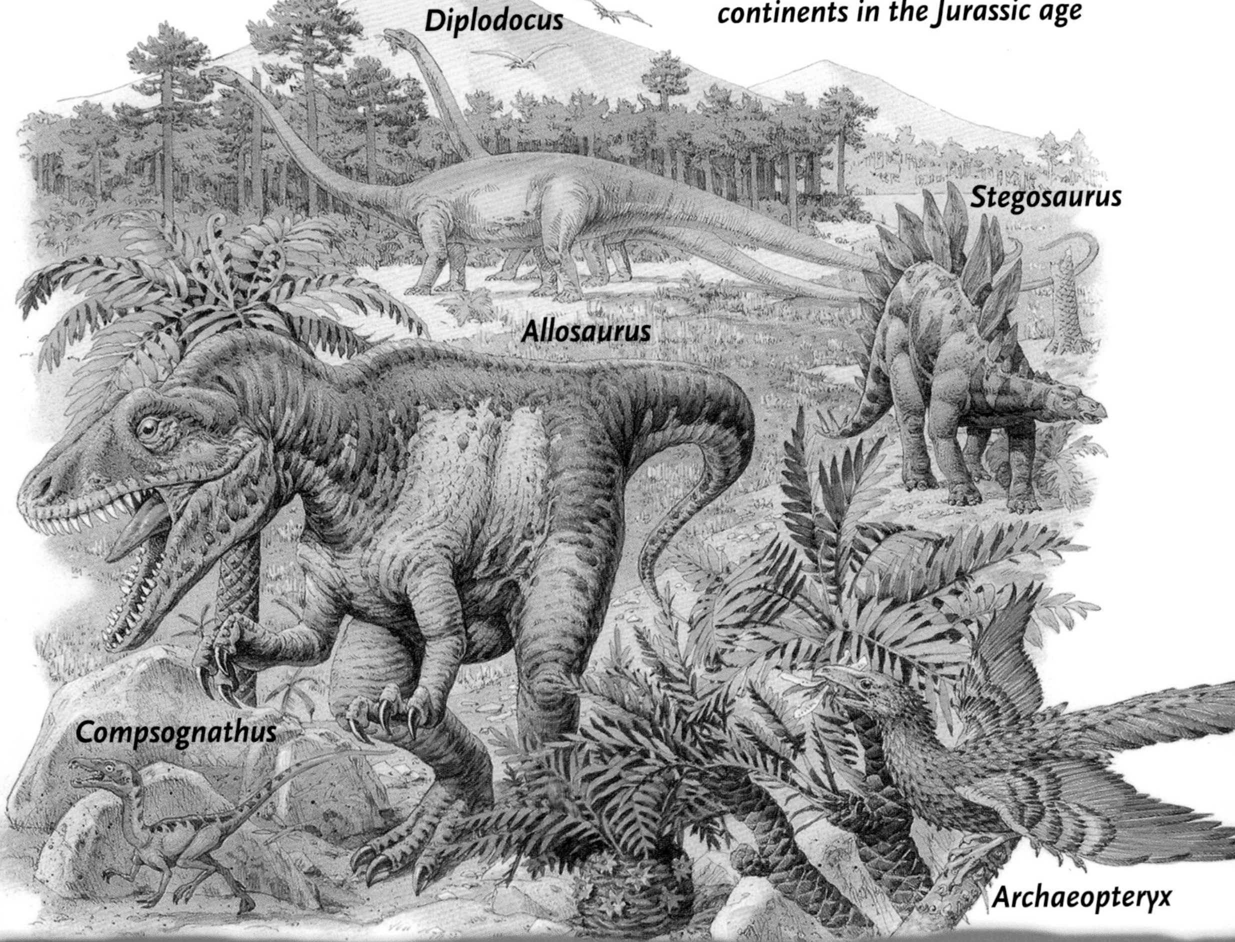

TWO DINOSAUR GROUPS

Hundreds of dinosaur species lived on Earth. There were two groups: saurischians ("lizard-hipped") and ornithischians ("bird-hipped"). There were two kinds of saurischians: meat-eating, bipedal (two-legged) theropods, and the plant-eating sauropodomorphs, which walked on either two or four legs.

These groups were defined by the shape and position of the hip bones. An ornithischian's pubic bone (above) slanted backwards. The pubic bone of a saurischian (right) pointed forwards.

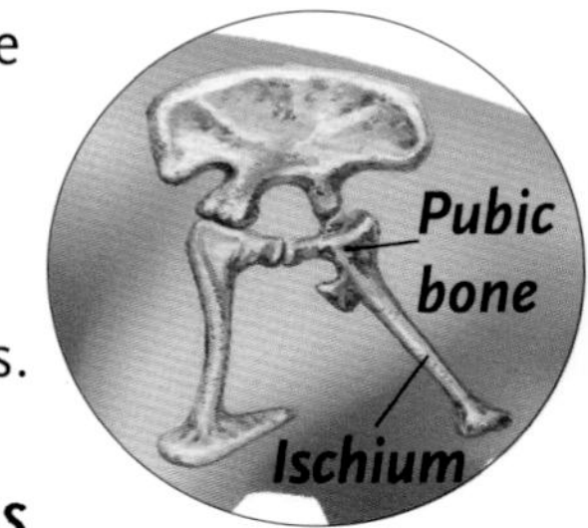

SAURISCHIANS

Most Sauropodomorphs had long necks and tails. Prosauropods (1) were once thought to be the bipedal ancestors of four-legged sauropods (2), but they are now considered separate groups. The theropods were the first dinosaurs to evolve. Their upright stance gave them the advantage of speed over other reptiles. The theropods were made up of ceratosaurs and tetanurans: long-clawed therizinosaurs (3), raptors (4), huge tyrannosaurs (5), and ornithomimids (6).

ORNITHISCHIANS

Thyreophoran dinosaurs included the stegosaurs (7), which had rows of plates or spines along their backs, and the ankylosaurs (8), which had armored bodies.

The scelidosaurs, a third group, may have been ancestors to both.

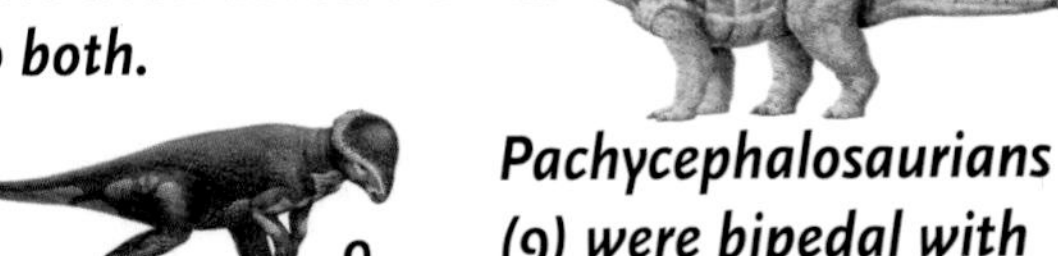

Pachycephalosaurians (9) were bipedal with thick skulls.

The ceratopsians (10) were large, four-legged dinosaurs with horns and neck frills.

The first ornithopods were small, bipedal hypsilophodonts. Later kinds included the larger iguanodonts (11) and the hadrosaurs or "duckbills." (12)

Rhamphorhynchus

ram-fo-RINK-us

RHAMPHORHYNCHUS was an early pterosaur. It had a small, furry body. Its wings were made of skin stretched between its long fourth finger and its back legs. Its long, stiff tail had a diamond-shaped tip. Inside its long, narrow jaws were sharp teeth, great for snatching frogs, fish, and bugs.

To catch its prey, Rhamphorhynchus flew low over rivers and seas, dragging its beak in the water like a scoop. Once it caught a fish, it tossed it into its throat pouch like a pelican would today. Its teeth pointed forward and outward, forming a cage to hold its prey.

PUFFIN HEAD

Dimorphodon (right) had a giant head that was deep and narrow like a puffin's. Males had colored beaks to impress females during mating rituals.

Rhamphorhynchus had a 3-ft (1 m) wingspan.

"BEAK SNOUT"

The name Rhamphorhynchus means "beak snout." The earliest-known pterosaurs were already advanced fliers by the Late Triassic period, 210 million years ago. Early pterosaurs from the Triassic and Jurassic periods had longer tails and shorter necks than later pterosaurs.

Batrachognathus, or "frog jaw," (above) had jaws lined with peg-like teeth. It was quick enough to catch dragonflies in flight. Its small size and short tail would have helped it to chase after them.

CLIFF HANGER

Rhamphorhynchus had a fifth toe and sharp claws, perfect for grasping branches and rocks. This suggested that it was probably an expert climber. When it was taking a rest from flying, it most likely spent its time hanging from cliffs. On the ground, the animal would have folded its wings, like birds and bats do today, and walked around on its tiny legs.

Dimorphodon most likely walked upright, like a bird, with its legs under its body. It could also run fast on its toes.

Rhamphorhynchus had huge eye sockets, so its eyes were probably very large. With such good eyesight, it could have spotted prey on land or at sea from high up in the air.

Pteranodon

PTERANODON was a pterosaur from the pterodactyl group. It had a furry body and a very short tail. Like other pterosaurs, its wings were made of skin stretching from its long fourth finger to its short back legs just above its webbed feet. It had a large, backward-pointing, bony crest on its skull.

Pteranodon lived on coasts and fed on fish it spotted from far away with its superb eyesight. Its long wings were kept stiff by long fibers inside the skin. These were called actinofibrils.

Pteranodon fossils have been found close together in groups, some with small crests, others with large ones. The smaller-crested reptiles were probably females.

Pteranodon sternbergi

Pteranodon probably ate like a pelican does today: it scooped up fish from the water's surface in its long, narrow jaws and stored them in its throat pouch.

Pteranodon's wingspan could be up to 30 ft (9 m).

MISTAKEN IDENTITY

The name Pteranodon means "wings and no teeth." Pteranodon is often mistakenly called "pterodactyl" but there is not actually an animal that goes by this name. It is just a general name for all short-tailed pterosaurs. Pteranodon was the largest-known pterosaur from the time it was first discovered in 1870 until 1975, when Quetzalcoatlus, an even bigger pterosaur, was found.

Ornithocheirus (above) was possibly the largest flying creature of all time. With a wingspan of up to 40 ft (12 m), it lived off the coasts of Europe and South America about 125 million years ago. It had a unique "keel" at the end of its toothed beak, useful for trapping fish.

WHAT'S THE CREST FOR?

No one really knows. It is possible that it helped keep the animal stable as it flew, or was used for steering or slowing down in flight. Pteranodon's head was large, so it could have acted as a counterweight to balance the heavy skull. It may also have been used by males, which probably had bigger crests than females, to impress mates during courtship, or to scare rival males away.

Pteranodon's long wings were perfect for gliding on ocean air currents, just as an albatross does today. It could travel for miles without flapping its wings.

Pteranodon longiceps had a wingspan of 23 ft (7 m).

Quetzalcoatlus

kwet-suhl-kuh-WAT-lus

LIKE other pterosaurs from the pterodactyl group, Quetzalcoatlus had a furry body, long narrow wings, a long neck, and a pointed beak. On its head was a short, bony crest. Its favorite foods were fish and shellfish. It also scavenged meat from other predators.

For its huge size, its skeleton was extremely light. Quetzalcoatlus may have weighed only about 220 lbs (100 kg).

MINI SCAVENGER

Pterodactylus (left) had a wingspan of 2 to 3 feet (61 cm—1 m) wide. Its tiny pointed teeth were good for chewing fish. Crawling around on all fours on land, it also scavenged meat from other animals' kills.

Huanhepterus (above) had a set of teeth like a sieve. It took water in its mouth and strained tiny creatures from it.

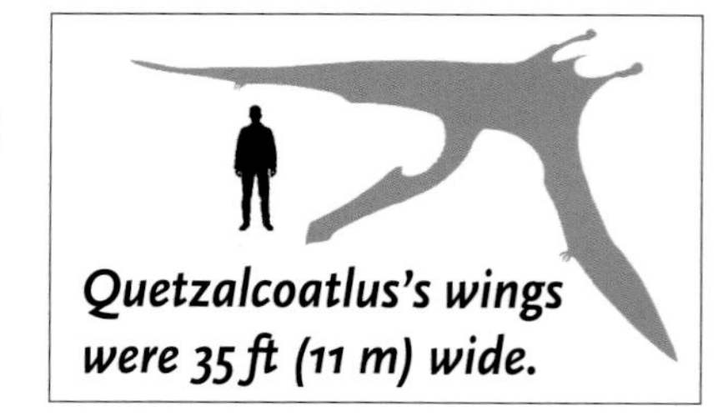

Quetzalcoatlus's wings were 35 ft (11 m) wide.

A TALL SNAKE GOD

Quetzalcoatlus was named after the Aztecs' feathered snake god, Quetzalcoatl. When it stood up, it was 18 feet (5 m) tall, about the height of a giraffe today. Quetzalcoatlus may have lived like a vulture, eating carcasses left behind by other carnivorous animals.

Gliding over the sea, it may have used its long, slim jaws to pluck fish from the water's surface, as a heron does today.

It lacked the muscle power to take off by running quickly. Instead it may have taken to the air by launching itself from a cliff edge.

Pterodaustro's lower jaw (above) had hundreds of bristles, good for straining tiny animals from the water.

Dsungaripterus (above) had a bony crest on its upward-curving beak.

Tupuxuara

Tapejara

Both Tapejara and Tupuxuara had sail-shaped head crests made of skin and held up by bone. These crests were probably used in displays to attract a mate.

Ichthyosaurus

ik-thee-uh-SAWR-us

ICHTHYOSAURUS was a marine reptile. Its body looked like a dolphin's. It had a slim, pointed snout with conical teeth, a fish-like tail, and a fin on its back. Its front flippers were twice the size of the back ones. Its nostrils were near its eyes, rather than at the tip. Ichthyosaurus lived close to the surface of the sea, eating fish and shellfish.

Ichthyosaurus is one of the few prehistoric animals whose fossils show evidence of skin color. Ichthyosaurus's skin was dark red or brown, and without scales.

Mixosaurus, 3 ft (1 m) long, and 25-foot (8 m) long Shonisaurus were members of the ichthyosaur family.

Fossils of Ichthyosaurus show the finger bones inside its flippers.

Complete fossils, many in perfect condition, have been discovered. Some are of pregnant mothers. You can see the bones of their babies inside.

Ichthyosaurus was about 6 ft (2 m) long.

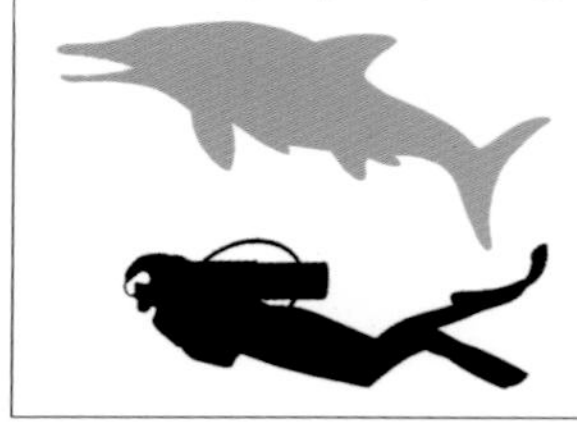

WATER BABIES

The name Ichthyosaurus means "fish lizard." Its young were born live. They came from their mother tail first, just as whale calves do today. Baby Ichthyosauruses could swim right after they were born. Fossils show that most pregnant Ichthyosauruses had only two babies at a time, though they could have as many as 11.

Eurhinosaurus's upper jaw was long and narrow with teeth pointing sideways.

WHAT BIG EYES YOU HAVE!

Temnodontosaurus (above) was an ichthyosaur from the Early Jurassic period. It was a gigantic animal, growing up to 40 feet (12 m) long. Its eyes measured about 8 inches (20 cm) across, the largest of any vertebrate (an animal with a backbone) that ever lived. These eyes would have been its main way to find prey deep underwater.

Ammonites, Ichthyosaurus's favorite food, were sea creatures with shells like a snail's. Related to today's squid and octopuses, they caught their tiny prey with their long tentacles.

Plesiosaurus

plee-zee-uh-SAWR-us

PLESIOSAURUS was a marine reptile with a long neck, a short tail, and a small head. It had many cone-shaped teeth. Its nostrils were on top of its head. It had long, narrow flippers, but no fins. Its body was covered with smooth (not scaly) skin. It ate fish, squid, and shellfish in surface waters.

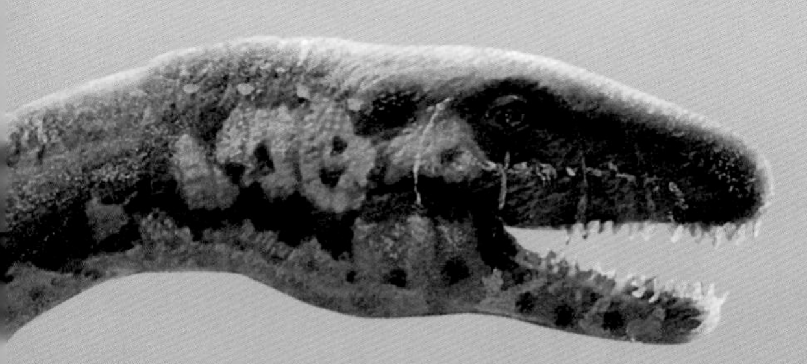

Plesiosaurus's lower jaw could open very wide. Its sharp, interlocking teeth were a good fish trap.

Macroplata (above left) lived in shallow seas off the coast of Europe during the Early Jurassic period. A relative of Plesiosaurus, it had large, powerful shoulders and a long neck.

Plesiosaurus was 15 ft (5 m) long.

Plesiosaurus used its long neck to reach forward and snatch small marine creatures in its jaws.

A SWIMMING LIZARD

"Plesiosaurus" means "near lizard." It was given this name to show it was more closely related to land reptiles than marine reptiles. Its flippers each contained five fingers made up of many smaller bones. It may also have laid eggs on land, like sea turtles do today.

Elasmosaurus's neck was more than half its total body length.

FOUND: LOCH NESS MONSTER?

Could the Loch Ness Monster—if it exists at all—really be a plesiosaur? Probably not. First, lakes are too cold for such a large, cold-blooded animal to survive. Second, plesiosaurs needed to breathe air regularly, which would mean that many more people would have seen "Nessie."

Paleontologists once thought a plesiosaur's flippers were like large oars, moving back and forth as it swam. Now scientists think they were more like wings flapping up and down. The bones in these flippers were more like a penguin's or a sea turtle's, which both "fly" through water.

A long neck was good for reaching up from deep water to catch fish by surprise. It could also help a plesiosaur change direction quickly as it swam while hunting. It probably could not lift its head too far above the water's surface. Its head and neck were too heavy.

Kronosaurus

kroh-nuh-SAWR-us

Kronosaurus's sharp, forward-pointing front teeth were perfect for trapping prey. Its back teeth were good for crushing bones and shells.

KRONOSAURUS was a pliosaur (a short-necked plesiosaur) that lived in warm, shallow Jurassic seas. An extremely powerful predator, it hunted anything that swam, including other marine reptiles. Its giant head was about a quarter of its body length. It had four paddle-like flippers for swimming and a short, pointed tail. Its front flippers were almost as long as a person is tall.

Kronosaurus's head was bigger than that of Tyrannosaurus rex!

Kronosaurus was 30 ft (9 m) long.

GREATEST OF ALL TIME

Kronosaurus's name means "lizard of Chronos." Chronos was the ancient Greek god of time who ate his five children as they were born in order to keep power for himself.

Kronosaurus was probably the biggest marine reptile that ever lived. It "flew" through the water using its four paddle-like flippers, just as sea turtles do today. It may also have laid its eggs in nests on land as sea turtles do, using its powerful flippers to drag itself ashore.

LIFE AT SEA

Many species adapted to life in the water. Platecarpus and Tylosaurus were both mosasaurs (sea lizards). Platecarpus ate fish and tiny ammonites, but giant Tylosaurus had a bigger appetite. It fought with Xiphactinus over bigger prey such as large fish, marine reptiles, and sea birds.

Archelon was the largest-known sea turtle, measuring 13 feet (4 m) long. Like a leatherback turtle today, its "shell" was a bony frame covered with skin.

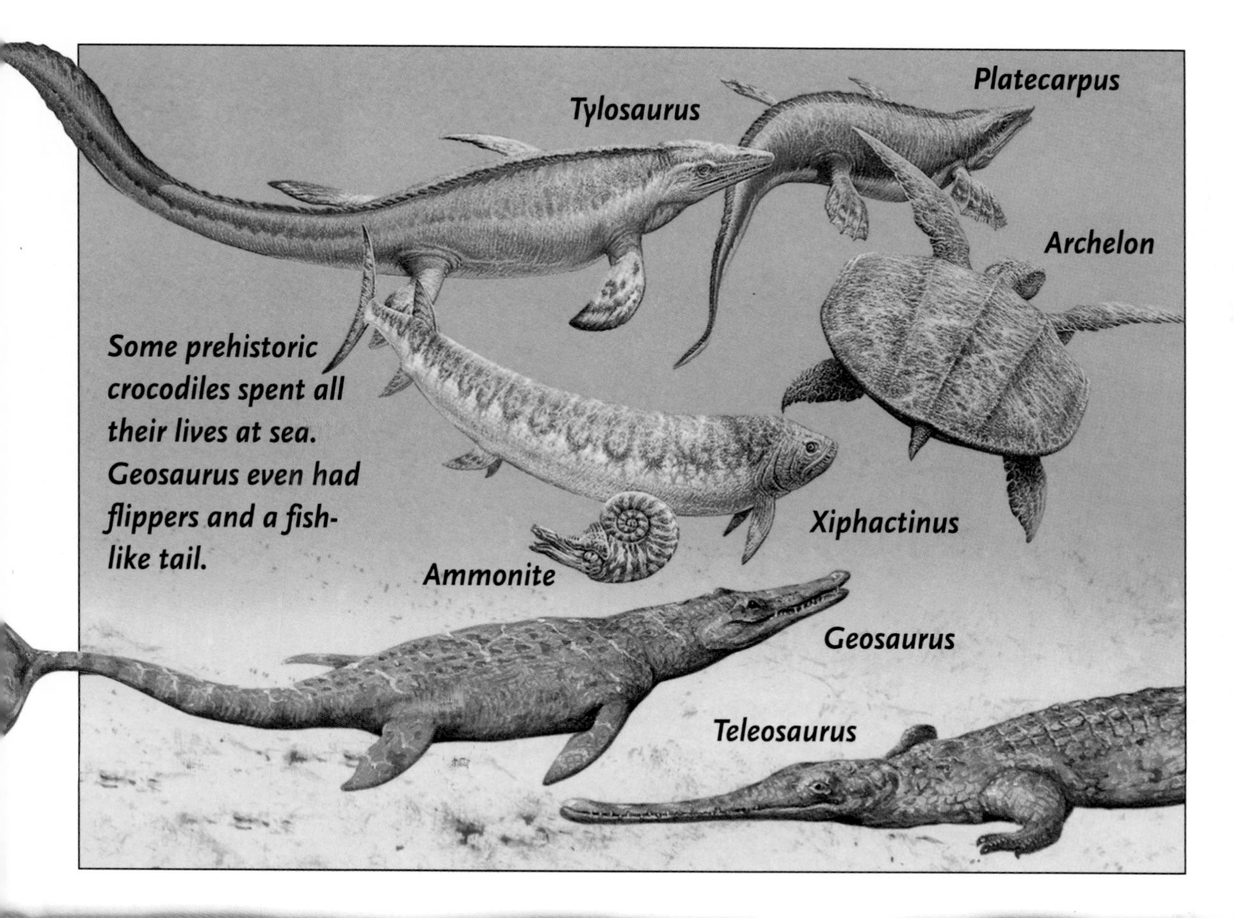

Some prehistoric crocodiles spent all their lives at sea. Geosaurus even had flippers and a fish-like tail.

Glossary and Index

amphibians (am-FIH-bee-unz) Animals that live much of their lives on land, but which have to return to water to breed.

archosaurs (AHR-kuh-sawrz) A group of reptiles that first appeared in the late Permian period, and were the ancestors of crocodiles, pterosaurs, dinosaurs, and birds.

dinosaurs (DY-nuh-sawrz) Reptiles that lived on land 230-65 million years ago and walked upright on legs held beneath their bodies.

fossil (FO-sul) The remains of an animal or plant preserved in rock. A living thing becomes fossilized when buried by sediments and the spaces within its tissues are filled by minerals which set hard over time.

pelycosaurs (PEH-lih-kuh-sawrz) A group of prehistoric reptiles, some of which had large sails of skin supported by bone sticking up from their backs.

plesiosaurs (PLEE-see-uh-sawrz) Marine reptiles with long necks, small heads, and large, paddle-like flippers.

pterosaurs (TER-uh-sawrz) Flying reptiles with wings that were formed from skin flaps between their fourth finger and lower body.

Page numbers in **bold** refer to illustrations